Blessings in the
DARK

*Even when you think
God is not there,
He is . . .*

OGUGUA PATRICIA AJAYI

First Edition, 2019
ISBN: 978-1-77605-594-4
ISBN: 978-1-77605-593-7 (e-book)

Layout & typesetting by Janet Von Kleist
jvonkleist@yahoo.com

Published by Kwarts Publishers
www.kwartspublishers.co.za

The story, all names, characters, and incidents portrayed in this book are fictitious. No identification with actual persons (living or deceased), is intended or should be inferred.

To the Almighty God, giver of all good things,
the source of all inspiration and my Father.
May the words of my mouth and the meditations
of my heart be acceptable in your sight always.

Chapter 1

Ella Martins,
Lekki Roundabout

LAGOS

The red SUV inched slowly along the Lekki phase 1 traffic. The weather was typical for Lagos; the sun was shining brightly, and the heat was stifling. Car horns were blaring, seemingly at no one in particular, and street traders could be seen hawking their goods and trying desperately to catch the attention of potential customers slowly passing by in their cars. The mixture of sounds seemed like loud continuous music, without rhythm. The traders sold everything under the sun: foodstuffs, electronic gadgets, books, CDs, and DVDs.

The hustle and bustle of the city was tangible, with pedestrians walking briskly and purposefully to their destinations. Mass transit buses were everywhere, with passengers jumping out before the buses came to a complete halt. A fight had broken out among the occupants of two vehicles by a corner; people were shouting at one another. Everyone seemed to be on steroids. The heat could make one antsy. Lagos chaos at 1.00 pm was at its peak.

The SUV moved slowly around the bend, its air conditioning insulating its occupants from the sweltering heat outside. Ella was driving, and her kids were in the back seat, their tight seatbelts restraining them like dogs on a leash. Soft music came from the car speakers. The mood inside the car contrasted sharply with the atmosphere outside.

"Daddy is coming home tomorrow!" the children chanted in excitement.

The two brothers looked almost identical, but one was obviously older than the other. They were handsome boys with broad foreheads and deep-set brown eyes. The older boy, Femi, was ten years old and had a deep cleft on his chin. His friends teased him about it, but his father always told him that the cleft was a mark of intelligence and character. He had been named after his father, Femi Martins, and everyone called him Femi Junior or FJ. His younger brother, Tope, was chatting excitedly. Tope was six years old, the baby of the family and that position came with perks. Tope knew this and didn't shy away from taking advantage of his position.

Ella glanced at the rear-view mirror and smiled at her sons. Ella was a very pretty lady, plus size with light brown skin, large brown eyes, and long lashes. She loved to laugh, a typical extrovert, the life of the party. Ella had such a big heart that it was difficult not to love her. She was as kind as she was bubbly. She put everyone first. Her family loved her immensely, and she loved them right back.

Ella was just as excited as the boys. She hadn't seen her husband, Femi, in over a month, and she missed him so much. He was finally coming home! She went over her plans in her mind again; he was going to arrive in the morning, and after the kids had their fill of him, she was going to attend to him, wait on him, and serve him anything he wanted. She loved him! He was a good man. She hoped she wouldn't feel too tired and exhausted because she had been battling a persistent headache over the last few days. *Oh well, I'm sure it's because I've been so busy*, she thought to herself. *Once Femi gets home, I will be able to rest.* At the moment she was pain-free and happy. Her thoughts were interrupted by the loud voices of Femi and Tope chanting. She joined in, "Daddy is coming home tomorrow!" All was right in the world, and she was happy.

The traffic lights at the junction turned green, and she started to move the car forward. Suddenly she felt a sharp pain in her forehead. *What was that?* A bolt of red light quickly flashed in her line of vision. It cleared up pretty quickly, so she thought she had imagined it. Then the headache came again, stronger this time. Now she was very scared. *What is happening to me? Oh God, please help me!* She was alone in the car with the kids. She knew she had to stop the car. She thanked God for the slow traffic, began to edge out of the lane, and turned on her indicator lights.

She carefully put the car in park, bowed her head, and prayed to God, "Father, help my children, help Femi," and everything became black. Silence . . .

FJ was the first to notice that his mother was not moving.

"Mummy, mummy!" he exclaimed, "What's the matter? Why did you park?" His voice held a little note of apprehension. His mum was not responding. He reached forward and shook her shoulder forcefully. "Mummy, why did you stop the car? Are you sleeping?"

When Ella did not respond, he began to panic. He had turned ten years old a few months back, and his mum had told him he would be in charge whenever she or daddy were not available. His mind began racing. *What am I going to do? Mummy said to call Aunty Tinuke in the event of an emergency.* Instinctively, he unbuckled his seatbelt and scrambled out of the car. He opened the car's front door, feeling confused as he stared at his mother's lifeless body. The car engine was still running. FJ shook Ella vigorously while shouting "Mummy!" but got no response. In desperation, he leaned over his mother to get her bag. He fumbled through it looking for her phone. There were so many things in there.

"Where is mummy's phone?" he muttered under his breath.

By this time, Tope had noticed that something wasn't right and began to cry.

"What is happening to mummy? Mummy! Muuumyyyy!" he screamed. This heightened Femi's anxiety. He was acting on autopilot. He began to shake his mother once again.

"Mummy, I can't find your phone!" he cried out in anguish. He held on to hope for an answer. He shook her again, desperation in his voice. "Mummy, please wake up, I can't find your phone . . . how will I call Aunty Tinuke?" He began to sob uncontrollably.

Tope joined his brother outside the car crying and calling for mummy to wake up.

Chapter 2

Wale Ojo, Lekki Roundabout

LAGOS

W ale Ojo, a successful businessman in his late 30s, was sitting in the back seat of a chauffeur-driven sedan. Well-groomed, wearing an expensive shirt, Wale had been engrossed in a business report he was reviewing and happened to glance up when he noticed the strange scene on the side of the road ahead of him. The traffic was slow, and he wondered why no one else seemed to notice the red SUV. The front door of the SUV was open, with two children looking dazed and confused, sobbing uncontrollably. There was a lady slumped on the steering wheel. *Oh my God*, he thought. *Could it be an alcoholic? A heart attack?* His heart began to pound in his chest as his car inched closer to the SUV. He was agitated and irritated by the seeming nonchalance of people passing by. On the other hand, he was acutely aware of ingenious techniques used by carjackers to lure unsuspecting good Samaritans into a trap. He became apprehensive as he ordered the driver to park the car.

Wale got out and walked cautiously toward the SUV, looking for any signs of foul play. The sobbing boys were still standing by the open driver's door, looking lost and confused. The scene was heart-breaking. An elderly couple was crossing the road and were also approaching the vehicle. Wale arrived at the car at the same time. The two boys were clinging to their mum, who was slumped over the steering wheel. The elderly lady reached out to pull the younger boy into her arms while FJ tried to explain, almost incoherently "Mummy isn't waking up! I have to call Aunty Tinuke, but I can't find mummy's phone in her bag."

Wale gently moved FJ aside and leaned over to shake Ella's shoulder. She was completely motionless. He couldn't smell alcohol. The gravity of the situation suddenly hit him.

Wale took his phone out of his jacket pocket and with trembling fingers, he dialled his personal assistant, Clara.

"Get an ambulance," he said sharply when Clara answered.

"Are you okay, sir?" The voice crackled at the other end of the line.

"I am alright! Just do as I say! Get them to send an ambulance to the Lekki phase 1 estate roundabout. A lady is in trouble! There is a Red SUV parked at the side of the road. Hurry!"

At this point, people were beginning to gather. Wale was relieved that an ambulance would be on its way shortly. His office had a retainer agreement with a hospital in the area. He had never needed to use the hospital service before, and he hoped they were efficient. While Wale was on the phone, the older gentleman tried to see what he could do to help Ella. He unbuckled her seat belt, leaned her back into the seat, and put his fingers on her wrist. He could feel a weak pulse, but apart from that, she was still.

Wale stood beside the car looking wearily at the gaping crowd and feared for the safety of the kids. The older boy was still crying and insisting he had to call Aunt Tinuke. Bending down to speak to FJ, Wale asked, "Can you give me your Aunty Tinuke's phone number?"

"I don't know it by heart," the boy replied, sobbing. "It's on Mummy's phone."

"Where is your mummy's phone?" Wale asked gently.

FJ sniffed and wiped his eyes. "It's in my mum's bag, but I can't find it." As FJ was speaking, Wale could hear in the distance, slightly drowned by the loud voices in the crowd, the siren of an ambulance approaching. *What? The ambulance showed up so fast!* He heaved a sigh of relief and thanked God under his breath. He had to think fast. *What next?*

Wale knew he couldn't leave the boys or their mum alone. He ran back to his car and told the driver to turn the car around and join him. He picked up his wallet and ran back to the SUV as the ambulance arrived. Two paramedics in the ambulance jumped out and tried to create a path through the crowd for the ambulance to access the scene. Onlookers were taking videos and pictures and struggling for the best view. The ambulance officials seemed frustrated and were shouting instructions to the crowd, but their voices could hardly be heard above the noise of the crowd. The paramedics approached the car and assessed the woman, taking her pulse and checking her heartbeat.

Wale suddenly became aware that the boys had been clinging to him and screaming "Mummy, please don't die!"

In the confusion, he hadn't noticed that, unconsciously, he too had been clinging to them as well. Wale was not a praying man, but he found himself praying to God. "God, please help!" he repeatedly muttered as he watched the paramedics attending to the woman. The reality of the situation was too much for him to bear. A million thoughts raced through his mind. *How could this happen to these young kids?* he thought as he prayed. He looked down at the kids and realised he had been praying out loud. The boys were glancing at their mum and then at Wale, seemingly looking for some explanation as to what was going on.

The paramedics gently placed Ella on the stretcher and put her in the ambulance. One of the paramedics walked toward Wale and the kids.

"We are told these are the children of the patient. What is your relationship with them, please? Are the boys with you?"

Wale made a split-second decision. Yes, it was crazy, yes, it was none of his business, but he knew he couldn't leave these boys and go back to his life like nothing had happened. He felt an attachment to the boys that he could not explain. *I can't leave these boys. They are vulnerable. Anyone could take advantage of them, or worse, harm them.*

He heard himself respond, "Yes, they're with me."

"Alright sir," the paramedic said. "Do you have a car to follow us with?"

Wale nodded.

That was when Wale Ojo's life changed forever.

Chapter 3

The Waiting Room, Lekki Hospital

LAGOS

Wale got the boys into his car and ordered his driver to follow the ambulance. He looked beside him and saw FJ clutching tightly to his mum's bag. *Smart little fellow*, Wale thought, *He had the presence of mind to grab the bag in all that confusion.* Tope had fallen asleep in exhaustion, whimpering in his sleep for Mum.

Suddenly, FJ looked up and said, "We must call Aunty Tinuke."

"Okay, we will," Wale responded.

Wale paused and asked, "Do you have a dad?" He wondered how such an obvious question could have slipped his mind.

"Yes," FJ replied. "He is coming back tomorrow. He has been abroad for the past month."

Wale's heart sank. *These boys are really alone.* He was turning over the events in his mind as he watched the ambulance come to a screeching halt at the hospital. He had never needed to use this hospital, and this was Wale's first time here. As he and the boys got out of the car, he looked up at the massive building. He closed the door and walked toward the hospital while the paramedics wheeled Ella in through the emergency entrance. He quickened his pace with the kids in hand so as not to lose track of the paramedics. The hospital seemed to be state of the art, and he felt reassured that he had made a good choice in calling his personal assistant.

The atmosphere seemed surreal. The crowds were gone. It was only Wale and the children. The guards at the emergency entrance let them in as he looked around and motioned to his driver to park and wait for him. When he turned back, he realised he couldn't see where the paramedics had taken the woman. A guard noticed his confusion and pointed toward a large door. Wale hurried toward the door, holding the boys' hands tightly. As he pushed the door open, he saw some nurses wheeling the stretcher into a room marked "Emergency". Wale tried to enter the room, but was stopped by hospital personnel, who ushered them into a waiting area. Wale took the boys to a row of seats against the wall, feeling slightly exhausted. The boys clung to him like their lives depended on it.

As he settled down to gather his thoughts, Wale heard a faint beep.

Tope cried out, "Mummy's phone!" pointing to the bag FJ was still clutching.

FJ dug into the bag, searching frantically, but didn't seem to make any progress. Wale took the bag from FJ's clumsy hands and turned it upside down, its contents tumbling out. *Women and their bags*, he thought in amazement. There was everything in this bag save the kitchen sink. Then hooray!

They saw the phone! Luckily it was still ringing. He noticed the name on the screen: AUNTY TINUKE.

"Phew," he sighed with relief. He quickly accepted the call and passed the phone to FJ, who was stretching his hand out for the phone. Wale wondered how he would have been able to decode any password the lady may have set up to reach her contacts if this call hadn't come in. Wale could hear the conversation from FJ's side.

"Aunty Tinuke! Aunty Tinuke," he cried. "It's Mummy! Mummy isn't waking up!" FJ was almost inaudible as he burst into tears whilst talking. Wale took the phone from him to salvage the situation. He could hear a female voice on the other side of the line, almost screaming,

"What happened to Ella!? What happened to your mummy?!"

Wale introduced himself. "Hello, my name is Wale. The boy's mum went into a kind of coma at the roundabout getting into Lekki phase 1 estate. The car was parked at the side of the road when I met them. I called an ambulance and brought them to the hospital." Crying hysterically, Tinuke asked for the hospital address.

"I will be there as quickly as I can. I am about an hour away," she said. "Thank you for what you did. God bless you. You must be an angel."

Wale hung up and shook his head, muttering, "Angel? I am no angel."

Chapter 4

Kishi Town, Oyo State

NIGERIA

It was a cool evening in the generally quiet village of Kishi. The setting was quite picturesque. There was an expanse of unrestricted foliage, with palm trees, fruit trees, and hibiscus plants everywhere rooted in the red earth. Small bungalows were scattered around the neighbourhood. Villagers milled around and outside their homes, men in clusters talking about the day. Mothers were calling their children in for the evening meal.

The setting was besmirched by a scene happening not too far away, around the village dump. A young Wale, just a teenager, was hanging out with a group of rambunctious friends, smoking something wrapped in leaves. Beer bottles were scattered all around them. They stopped their loud chatter when a woman's shout could be heard getting louder.

"Waaaaaale! Wale, where are you?"

One of the young boys ducked behind the dumpster they were all hanging around just as an old lady walked around the corner. Her eyes were teary, and she looked exhausted. She was slightly bent and had a head of white hair partly covered in her traditional scarf. A look of heavy disappointment crept into her eyes as she recognized her grandson's friends.

"Where is Wale, my son?" she asked dejectedly, looking at each of them with a slight hint of compassion. *They are just children. They shouldn't be doing this.* Well, she couldn't help all of them, but she would never stop trying to get her only grandson back on the right track.

"We have not seen Wale since Morning, ma," the boys answered untruthfully, a few of them looking away, but the majority staring straight at her.

She knew they were lying, and they knew she knew, but they didn't care.

She sighed, turned to walk away, and said, "Tell him to please come home."

"Yes Ma," they replied.

As soon as the woman left, not even waiting to make sure she was out of hearing distance, the boys burst into raucous laughter. Wale came out from behind the dumpster, upset that his grandma had once again made him a laughing stock in front of his friends. *What is wrong with that old woman? Why does she pester me so much?*

"Waaaaaale," his friends continued to tease. "Wale baby, come and eat. Wale baby, have you brushed your teeth?"

Wale was livid and embarrassed, but hid it well as he bluffed to his friends.

"One day I'll leave that house and never come back! She gets on my last nerve! I wish she would just die and leave me be!" he said passionately.

"Why wait for her to die?" the self-acclaimed leader of the group, Bayo, asked as he got up from an old car tire he had been sitting on. Bayo was a young man with deep scars all over his body, each scar telling a story of the horror he had endured and the pain he had equally inflicted on others. He had lived a terrible life in his short years on Earth. He had been exposed to untold revulsions as a child, and now he lived just to replicate the nightmare on others. You could almost say he had no soul left. He repeated slowly, his meaning crystal clear as he approached Wale ominously,

"Why wait for her to die?" With a coarse voice he asked, "Wale, why not do something about it now?"

There was silence in the group as the full implication of what their leader had insinuated sank in. "Wale, you heard me," Bayo said with his voice slightly raised. "Don't complain; do something about it."

Wale began to tremble and asked a question, dreading the answer.

"What can I do about it?"

Bayo snarled, "Finish her, kill her! Take your destiny into your own hands. If she is a problem, get her out of your way, or we will do it for you." There was an evil glint in his eyes.

"For me?" Wale gulped.

"Yes, for you," Bayo continued. "We are a brotherhood, we stand together, and we will never leave you."

Wale became afraid. How did he get himself into this situation?

"Kill her? How?" he stammered. "How?"

"That's easy," Bayo replied. "We just walk over to your house and give her a good shaking up; she won't last long. Just one blow to the back of her skull will do the job, and then you'll be free! Free to live your life the way you want." There was a brief pause, and then he sneered, "This will be your test, Wale. You always said you wanted to be respected in this group, so show us what you can do."

Wale was frozen to the spot. Yes, he wanted to be respected; he desired to belong, but not like this. All through his life he had always felt rejected, first by his own father who had walked out on him and his mother when he was just two years old, leaving them to suffer terribly. Then he had been rejected by his mother, who decided when he was seven years old that it was easier to kill herself than go on existing with him. What kind of mother does that? Of course, Grandma had tried to explain that it wasn't his fault and that his mum suffered from a mental illness. Wale never understood and didn't care about all that. They were just excuses to hide the truth. They hadn't wanted him. How unlovable was he? How terrible could he be to be rejected by the very people who had brought him into this world, and who had decided that life with him wasn't worth living?

Wale had always had a desire to belong somewhere. He had carried this weight of being unwanted all his life. It had affected his time in school. He was always moody and sullen and refused to make friends; he was defiant and a rebel. No one bothered with him except his grandmother. She repeatedly said she loved him and wouldn't leave him, but how could he ever believe her? When this group of degenerates had asked him to join their group, he couldn't believe his luck. Somebody wanted him. He had been chosen. It was a brotherhood for life--at least that is what they had told him. Despite his grandmother's frequent warnings about hanging out with them, he stuck with the group. They were his family! But suddenly, they didn't seem like family. They looked evil and cruel. His Grandmother's warnings and premonitions began to replay in his head loud and clear. *Were they joking?! Kill his Grandma?! The only person alive who cared whether he lived or died?* In an instant, he saw her constant nagging and concern for what it was, true love! His grandmother loved him. Why had he not realised this before now? He began to shake uncontrollably. He was deeply afraid. The situation was spiralling out of control very fast.

Bayo growled, "Make up your mind, or we will make it up for you."

Wale remained silent.

With a snap of his fingers, Bayo got everyone's attention and said, "Come on guys, let's help our brother out. Let's rid him of his burden once and for all."

The other boys began to chuckle and laugh. They all seemed possessed, and it seemed the thought of hurting someone gave them such a high.

Wale was still frozen on the spot. He watched them pick up bottles, stones, pieces of metal until all of them had a weapon. They followed Bayo and headed to his home. Wale looked but could not move. He watched with horror as they all howled in ecstasy and began racing toward his home. "NOOOOOOOOOOOO!" He thought he was screaming, but no sound had come out of his mouth. He didn't understand why his body was not obeying him. He felt sweat trickle down his back. He had to do something! He couldn't let them hurt his Grandma. But he couldn't move. *PLEASE, GOD, HELP ME!* He had never prayed in his life. God belonged to his Grandma and her friends, not him. But in that instant, he screamed the prayer in his head.

Suddenly, he fell on the floor as if just released from a tight hold. He was shaking, but he managed to get up, and he began to run. Wale ran as fast as he could on his unsteady legs like his life depended on it. He had always been a fast runner. He quickly arrived at his home, the home where his grandmother had loved him and patiently, single-handedly raised him after his mother died. As he approached, he saw his group of friends screaming and howling like hyenas at the moon as they filed out of his house. They looked crazy. Wale stopped in his tracks. Bayo came out of his house last, covered in blood. Wale watched in terror as they ran away into the bushes. He rushed in shouting for his grandma.

"Mama! MAMAAA!" he screamed.

He rushed into her room and saw her lying on the floor. Her head seemed to be at an awkward angle and there was blood everywhere. He couldn't see where the blood had come from. Wale screamed and fell to the floor beside her. He shook her shoulder.

"Mama! Please, mama, get up! Please, mama, I am so sorry. I am so sorry! Mama, please get up! Mama, I am so sorry, please forgive me. I did this to you. Mama, please get up!" Wale screamed. Grandma wasn't responding. He knew the neighbours would soon come, hearing him screaming. And sure enough, Mama Tope from next door walked in. She was one of his Grandma's very good friends. She hated Wale, and the feeling was mutual. He didn't like her nosey ways and the condescending language she used when she spoke to him, like he was less than a human being. She didn't like Wale because she thought his Grandma was too lenient with him and always stood up for him when he misbehaved, which was often. She used every opportunity she had when she and Wale found themselves alone to tell him how useless she thought he was, and she was sure that Wale was going to kill his Grandma with all the trouble he caused her.

Mama Tope came in and hurried to her dear friend's side. She knelt and tried in vain to rouse her, just as Wale had done a few minutes earlier. With tears in her eyes, she slowly rose up to her full height of 5 feet. She could have been seven feet tall, with the effect she had on Wale. She looked at him and yelled at the top of her voice.

"YOU have killed her! You have finally killed this woman that has given her life for you! Are you happy now? You are a MURDERER!" She declared this loudly with all the venom and disgust she could muster. It sounded like she had just spoken on behalf of God himself!

"GOD WILL NEVER FORGIVE YOU FOR THIS!" she spat.

Something inside Wale was suddenly extremely terrified, and he believed her words with all his heart. He staggered out of his grandma's room, half-blinded by tears, but still hearing Mama Tope's voice ringing... "MURDERER! MURDERER!"

Wale ran ...

Chapter 5

Femi Martins,
Sandton, Johannesburg

SOUTH AFRICA

F emi was bent over his computer, his eyes glued to the screen, typing away furiously. He was just putting the finishing touches on his report. It had been an interesting month, but he was anxious to get home. He missed his family dearly! This was the longest time he had ever been away from them, and it had been tougher than he had anticipated. He stopped typing, and his mind wandered off to his wife, Ella. He smiled. His wife had been his best friend for over 15 years. They had met in high school and became instant friends, but they didn't start a romantic relationship until they got to University. She had always been in his life and he had never been apart from her for more than a month. But this contract was a big one, and it would benefit them financially. With both boys growing, they wanted to move them to a private school, and that wasn't cheap. He sighed. His boys, his pride and joy.

He loved being a father. It was the most important role he had to play. It amazed him how fast the boys were growing, especially his firstborn, FJ. He saw a lot of himself in his sons and it humbled him. He wanted to be the best dad he could be for them.

Femi shook his head to escape this pleasant reverie, pushed his glasses up on his nose, and went back to work. The sooner he finished this report, the sooner he could pack and head off to the airport and be with his family. His phone buzzed, but he did not notice it. It buzzed again, so he checked. It was Tinuke, his wife's best friend. *Why would she be calling? Okay, I'll call her back once I'm done.* He felt his phone vibrate again. He checked and saw it was Tinuke again. *Hmmm . . . this cannot be casual.* His curiosity was piqued, so he picked up his phone

"Hello, Tinuke How are you?" Wale asked.

"I'm good, and yourself?" Tinuke replied.

"I'm great, Tinuke, trying to finish up my report so I can head for the airport. How is my family? When last did you see them?"

Tinuke was silent for a moment and then replied, "Femi, is Deji there?"

Deji was Femi's business partner and best friend. They had been friends since they were in primary school. Their families lived in the same neighbourhood. He knew everything about him, and they both loved the same things. So when Femi had decided to start a Robotics Engineering company, it had been natural to partner with Deji. Deji was a people person, a natural salesperson. He "could sell snow to Eskimos" and he loved the field of robotics just as much as Femi did. He was downstairs working with the Finance department to settle their bills before they headed back to the hotel, then finally to the airport to get home.

"Deji?" Femi asked, slightly puzzled "Deji is downstairs."

At that moment, Deji rushed in panting like he had run a marathon.

"What's the matter with you?" Femi asked him, looking shocked.

Deji was usually calm, cool, and collected, never frazzled, but now he was looking confused. "Tinuke just asked after you," Femi continued, turned back to his phone again. "Tinuke, I can't talk now, I have to run. Please, a kiss for my wife and tell her I can't wait to see her," said Femi. He glanced up and saw Deji's face, and knew in an instant that something was wrong.

Still holding the phone to his ear, he asked, "Deji, what's wrong? You look like you have seen a ghost."

He could hear Tinuke on the phone saying, "Femi, I have something to tell you."

Femi took his eyes off Deji and gave Tinuke his full attention.

Tinike continued, "I just called Ella's phone and spoke to FJ. He said they are in a hospital in Lekki. I spoke to a man there who says Ella must have passed out at the steering wheel. I am on my way there now. I should be there soon. The boys are okay."

Femi was caught in between processing the expression on Deji's face and Tinuke's account of what was happening. He could feel his head spinning.

"What in the world are you talking about?" he said, his voice raised. "What's going on!?"

Tinuke now sounded like she was crying. "It's Ella; she's unconscious. The doctors are with her now."

Femi couldn't wrap his head around it. His Ella? Coma? Hospital? He had just spoken to her a few hours ago and she was fine. The boys had been singing in the car. It couldn't be Ella. Ella was on her way home to prepare for his arrival. She had said so.

"Tinuke," he said when he finally found his voice, "what are you saying?"

Without waiting for an answer, he hung up and quickly dialled Ella's number. It rang, but there was no answer. Femi tried to squelch the panic threatening to overwhelm him as he had to dial again.

"No reason to panic," he muttered to himself, "This is all some sort of misunderstanding."

Finally, the phone call was answered on the other side, but it wasn't Ella's voice he heard, it was FJ. He took a deep breath. *It's okay,*" he thought to himself, *Ella is probably in the kitchen.*

"How are you, my boy?" he asked, as brightly as he could.

FJ replied, voice quivering, "I'm fine, daddy . . . but Mummy is sick . . . Daddy, Mummy wasn't waking up. I was shaking her, and she wasn't waking up. I pushed her arms, but she wouldn't wake up. I tried to call Aunty Tinuke, but I couldn't find Mummy's phone. The ambulance came, and a nice man took us. Daddy, please come. I'm so scared and Mummy has gone in . . ."

As FJ continued to narrate the events unfolding, Femi's mind froze. He was hearing his son's words, but he wasn't comprehending anymore. He couldn't move. *My Ella? It couldn't be. I spoke to her just after she picked the boys up from school.* Then the full force of what he was hearing hit him.

"My guy," Deji spoke for the first time since entering the office. "Calm down. It's going to be alright. I am trying to book a seat on an earlier flight, but the flights are all full. I am working on it, though. The bags are in the car, and a driver is ready to take us to the airport. I'll get you on a flight now, even if it's the last thing I do."

Deji held on to Femi tightly. Femi's mind was sifting through the information his best friend had just told him. "You've tried to get seats? A driver is waiting? How long have you known about this?"

Femi pushed Deji away from him to look at his face.

"I said, how long have you known?!" Femi shouted at his longtime friend. He was beyond angry. He seemed to be struggling to breathe and speak at the same time. His words came out as a growl. "You left me working while Ella needed me?"

Deji knew he was in trouble. "I am sorry Femi," he wavered as he tried to launch into a frantic explanation. He was so intent on trying to explain that he didn't see the blow coming. He felt it. As he fell backwards, two things crossed his mind one after the other. First, *wow, Femi is strong* and next, *my tooth!*

Deji had known it was not going to be easy breaking the news to Femi. He had been acquainted with many couples in his lifetime, but very few like Femi and Ella. They were the real deal. The love between them was exceptional. Femi worshipped the ground Ella walked on. He was committed to making her happy, and Ella felt the same way about Femi. Being in their presence was magical. Femi called Ella God's special gift to him. He always said that God had favoured him so much that he brought Ella into his life. So when Tinuke had called Deji to tell him about Ella's condition, he knew it wasn't going to be easy. He had told Tinuke to give him 45 minutes to pack their things and try to organize logistics before she called Femi to tell him. He loved Femi like his own brother and knew the next few hours would be tough. He had already forgiven him for the blow.

"I am so sorry, Femi. You can get upset with me all you want. Let's get into the car and start for the airport," Deji said, beckoning Femi toward the door. Femi was still fuming, but he knew his anger wasn't at his friend. His emotions were up in the air and he didn't know what to do.

"Okay," Femi said. "What about the report? I must get my things," he said distractedly.

He didn't really care at this point, though. Deji knew this and replied, "I have spoken to the MD, and he has agreed to give us a few days to conclude. Let's just get to the airport."

Deji opened the door and headed out first, with Femi right on his heels. His chest was hammering as they took the stairs two at a time, ignoring the elevators. A black Mercedes was parked right in front of the office building. Deji jumped in and Femi was too distraught to ask for any details. As they got into the car and sped off, Femi finally gave in to the emotions that had been raging, and he burst into tears. He didn't just cry; he howled like an animal in pain. Deji had known this was coming and he was ready. He held his best friend like a baby. As Femi wept, his sobs sounded like his heart was going to burst with the anguish. The driver looked in the rear-view mirror at his passengers. He had never seen a man cry like that and he wondered what could have happened. Femi began to call on God. He wasn't praying coherently, but Deji could make out the words, "God, please save her. Father have mercy on me, save her! Father have mercy on me!" On and on Femi moaned.

When Femi had calmed down a bit, Deji took his phone and began to make some calls. He called Femi's mum, fondly known as Aunty Deborah and told her what had happened.

"Ye Kpaa!" she exclaimed in her local dialect. "My enemies have come again! This will not happen. God did not tell me any of my children will die! Where is my son? Where is Femi?" She screamed into Deji's ear.

One could imagine the state Deborah was in, with her hands stretched out and hopping up and down like a typical Nigerian mum does when faced with bad news.

"Femi is here, Ma, but he can't talk right now," Deji replied.

Femi's mum said, "Please put the phone on speaker so he can hear my voice. He doesn't have to reply." Aunty Deborah began to pray. She prayed fervently, like only a mother can, for she loved Ella like her own daughter, and she loved her only son and Deji too. The only love she had that could surpass what she had for the three of them was the love she had for God. She was a new Christian, but Femi and Ella had been born again Christians for a while. They had given their lives to Christ on the same day, as teenagers, and they had not looked back since. Femi's mother had never been interested in being 'born again' after all, she was a committed member of a church, served on the Women's Committee and was a consistent giver in church. What else could God have needed from her? She always dismissed their new love for God as just youthful exuberance. Femi and Ella prayed for his mum to come to the saving knowledge of Christ every day.

God had answered their prayers a year earlier when she had attended a friend's church and heard the gospel in a new way, and she had been convicted. Realising that her contributions to the church did not equate to salvation, she finally surrendered to Christ and passionately followed him. Now it seemed her faith was being tested, and she was not going to just roll over and take it. Her God was too good for that. She prayed and prayed. Deji responded with the required "amen" and "amen." Femi could only mumble an "amen" or two in between his sobbing. He went on with his own litany of "Father God save her . . . Father, have mercy on me."

Femi's mum ended the prayer with a declaration of faith. "Ella will not die, but will live to declare the works of the LORD."

She told Deji that she would continue praying and she expected regular feedback. Deji promised to keep her updated.

Sometime after this, still en route to the airport, Femi was able to speak to his sons again. This time he was calmer and was able to encourage them to pray for Mummy. He told them Daddy was coming home as quickly as he could. As Deji listened, he wished he had the faith of his friend. He had long ago given up on God. In his mind, God had ceased to exist for him the day he had prayed for his Mum to survive her illness and God had decided not to listen to him. He figured God didn't listen to prayers and was too busy to care about human affairs, and this perception had influenced his life. If God was too busy for him, he wouldn't give God the time of day either.

Deji was at his wit's end. He had to get a seat on that flight leaving in two hours. The ride to the airport would usually take 30 minutes, but in the afternoon traffic, it could take longer. He tried to make as many calls as possible, calling in every favour he could think of to get him and Femi seats on the flight to Lagos. The airline officials couldn't make any promises. They just insisted they would try their best. Femi had grown silent beside him. Now he was just in a daze. Deji didn't know which was worse, Femi's trance-like state or his gut-wrenching sobs. They were about five minutes from the airport, so he knew he'd have to wake Femi.

"Femi . . . Femi . . . get up! We are at the airport," Deji said.

"Did we get the tickets?" Femi asked, jumping out of his confused haze.

"No, we have not," Deji replied, "but I'll do something."

"Do what?" Femi screamed. "Do what, exactly? How are you going to fix this?" Deji ignored Femi. "Are you hearing me, Deji?"

Femi was screaming at him hysterically, but then his face crumpled, and he began to cry. Intense sobbing and quivering whimpers ripped through him, filling the car with a terrible noise.

Deji didn't respond. He closed his eyes and whispered, tears running down his cheeks, "Femi, let's pray."

That was enough to stop Femi's tears. *Deji?? Wants to pray?* Deji closed his eyes, held Femi's hand, and prayed. 'If you really exist, please help us," that was all Deji could muster. But he meant it. For Femi and Ella's sake, he hoped God was listening. He got out of the car and began to offload their luggage.

Chapter 6

The Lekki Hospital

LAGOS

Wale knew these boys needed him. The more he interacted with them, the more he couldn't help but see the difference between their childhood and his. It was like night and day. He heard them talk about their Dad like he was a superhero. He listened to the conversations they had with their father when he called them a second time. Femi kept repeating how much he loved them and reassuring them that he was coming as quickly as he could. Wale listened in disbelief. He thought such wonderful family dynamics were found only in the movies. But here he was listening to a Dad openly declare his love for his boys and their Mum, and telling them to pray for their Mum.

As soon as their dad hung up, FJ and Tope stretched out their hands to Wale.

"What is happening?" he asked, as he reached out to grasp their hands in his.

FJ replied, "We have to hold hands to pray so God can see we agree. God has no choice but to answer our prayers once we agree." FJ said this with such faith. "Uncle Wale," he continued, "Please pray for us."

Wale stuttered; he didn't know what to say. "I had better not. For your own good." He thought to himself, *God may decide not to answer your prayers with me here.*

But he said quietly, "FJ, you should pray for your mum."

FJ began to pray, simple, childlike, and pure. He was talking as though God was his uncle or a close family friend. Wale envied the boy's innocence for a second, but he quickly got over it and said a quiet "Amen" once FJ had finished praying. Wale looked at these boys in wonder. In fact, the whole day had been a wonder for him. How did he get here? He knew stopping to help them must have been orchestrated by something bigger than himself. On any other day, he would have driven past without a second glance, his mind probably focused on some report or contract. Also, he wasn't a Good Samaritan; he had learned early on to mind his business and keep his nose down. So why had he stopped? He had no idea.

The older couple who had also stopped to help the boys at the scene had to leave. They asked Wale if he would stay with the boys, and he found himself agreeing to stay until their Aunty arrived. She had been calling every 15 minutes. She was rushing down from the mainland, and he couldn't leave until she got there. He made a call and told his secretary to cancel all of his appointments for the rest of the day. He and the boys had snacks, and Tope was now asleep on his lap. Wale didn't have kids and had never even considered having any. He couldn't imagine reproducing and exposing a poor innocent child to being cursed with his bad blood. Besides, he hadn't met anyone he would have even wanted to date.

Wale was an enigma. He was rich, extremely handsome according to the tabloids, an astute businessman, and an all-around success story. But still, no one could say they knew him personally. He had no friends outside the office. He never drank any alcohol. He never had women around him, even though there was always a flock of willing women throwing themselves at him. He continuously and politely refused their 'not-so-subtle' advances. He knew there was a rumour in his office that he was gay. He laughed at the idea. They couldn't be more wrong. The problem was that the part of him that made human connections on a personal level had ceased to exist the day his grandmother had died practically by his own hands. He knew he had killed her. He couldn't risk anyone getting close enough to him to find out that he never slept more than three hours straight without having a nightmare. Nightmares that left him drenched in sweat and sometimes tears. He was constantly tormented by that day, even though it was more than a decade ago. The guilt sometimes was so strong it was like his heart was being squeezed lifeless. He was in deep anguish. It seemed with every financial break he got and every dollar added to his account made him feel even more guilt. He knew a great judgment was coming for him one day. And it was going to be terrible. God didn't take murder lightly.

Wale couldn't allow his sins to affect anyone else; let judgment be his and his alone. But now, looking at these boys, something tugged at his heart. With these thoughts on his mind, he looked up as he heard the glass door of the waiting room open and his heart literally skipped a beat. He saw the most amazing creature hurrying in. He had never seen anything like her. She was tiny, at least compared to him, she was. She had a round face with the biggest eyes he had ever seen. Her braids hung around her face like a cloak. She had the smoothest caramel skin, and she was simply gorgeous despite droplets of sweat running down her face and her frazzled look. Her shirt had come half untucked from her slacks. She stood there barefoot, and in her hands were Louis Vuitton stilettos along with a Gucci bag. She was the most beautiful woman he had ever seen, but her forehead was creased with worry as she anxiously scanned the faces in the waiting room. He wished he could help her and take the fear off her face forever. *Wow, Wale, take it easy there.* He didn't know what it was, but something about this woman arrested him, and he sat upright in his seat, startling the little boys awake.

Suddenly, FJ cried, "Aunty Tinuke!"

Tinuke hurried toward them and opened her arms out as the boys rushed in for a hug, crying and trying to speak at the same time. *Aunty Tinuke? THAT was their Aunty Tinuke?* Wale had imagined an old older woman, not this paragon of beauty. His jaw dropped. This was the woman he had been on the phone with for the past two hours?

Hugging the boys tightly, Tinuke looked up. He seemed to go on forever; she almost had to tilt her head back just to make eye contact. He was all muscle, all six feet of him. She was temporarily robbed of speech. They looked at each other just staring until FJ said in a loud voice, "What is the matter with both of you?"

The trance was quickly broken, and they both chuckled nervously.

"Uncle Wale, this is Aunty Tinuke," said FJ, introducing both parties.

Wale couldn't help but smile at the serious way FJ had made the introductions.

"Pleased to meet you, Aunty Tinuke." Wale stretched out his hand for a shake, but this lady didn't take his outstretched hand. Instead, she shocked the grin off his face when she stepped into his arms and gave him a hug with all her might. She fit as if she belonged there.

She whispered into his shirt, "Thank you. Thank you so very much." Wale's mouth went dry.

Chapter 7

Atinuke, Loves Legacy Orphanage, Lagos

NIGERIA

" Hello. I am Atinuke Bello. Born of no one, daughter of no one." That was how Tinuke had introduced herself to Ella the first day they met. Ella was a new child who had just arrived at the Orphanage and 'Big Mummy,' had told – rather, instructed – Tinuke to make her feel welcome. *Welcome?* Tinuke had thought. *Who could ever want to be welcome here?* With more than 70 other children running about, Atinuke had toyed with the idea of escape several times, and now she was to make some else feel welcome? She would just be a hypocrite! But 'Big Mummy' must always be obeyed, and in no time she found herself introducing herself to this girl.

Tinuke scrutinized the newcomer in detail. She looked to be around Tinuke's age and she was rather pretty, Tinuke had to admit, slightly enviously. She even had a brand-new pair of shoes! Tinuke had never seen new shoes in all her 9 years at the orphanage. This girl had obviously had a good life. *Why in the world was she here?* Her hair was nicely braided. *Well, that will be cut soon,* Tinuke thought smugly to herself. The girl was plump in a cute way. *Poor girl. Big Mummy's two meals a day rule will sort out that extra pudge soon enough.* Tinuke thought Ella looked out of place at the orphanage. The only thing that looked remotely familiar was her eyes. They looked empty. She was sad, even at that age. Tinuke could recognize misery. She had seen it many times with new kids and a few older ones too. They looked so lost and so miserable. Tinuke decided there and then that she liked this chubby girl and she would try to be nice to her, for her sake.

"Why would you say that?" Ella looked directly at Atinuke in genuine puzzlement and in response to Tinuke's introduction.

"Born of no one, daughter of no one? Someone gave birth to you or you wouldn't be here. Where is your mother? Is she dead, like mine?"

Tinuke changed her mind. She didn't like this new girl after all. She was too nosy. She turned and walked away and left Ella standing there. Big Mummy would not be happy, but now Tinuke didn't care. She climbed up her favorite tree in the large playground and sat there, telling herself not to cry. She hated feeling sorry for herself and to her, tears were a waste of time. She had learned that over the years.

Little Tinuke had been abandoned at the gates of the Love Legacy orphanage when she was a baby. Nobody knew who dropped her there, so she had no idea who her parents were or where she was from. She was given a Yoruba name because she was abandoned in Lagos, a Yoruba speaking state. She always wondered why Big Mummy had named her Atinuke. In English, it meant, "taken care of from conception." Oh, the irony! Taken care of from conception, then abandoned? It was like a mockery of her existence. Big Mummy told her it had nothing to do with her parents. Big Mummy believed God had taken care of her from conception and guided her safely to the orphanage. Tinuke wasn't buying this story, but she knew she couldn't complain too much. She was well looked after. She was fed twice a day, and although she was clothed in hand me downs, at least she had clothes. Interestingly, these things didn't bother her as much as the feeling of not belonging.

Atinuke had never connected with anybody. Big Mummy had tried her best, but she was everybody's mummy and she was limited in what she could offer. Any hope Tinuke had of a family of her own gradually died as year after year people looking to adopt passed her up. They always thought she was cute, but when they realized she was much older than she looked, they all stepped back in shock.

She heard a lady tell her husband "No, darling, we don't want to adopt a dwarf, do we?"

So as the years passed by, Tinuke assumed there was something wrong with her and learned to hide her disappointment every Saturday when guests came. Eventually, she stopped showing up for "line up." That's what Big Mummy called the parade of the orphans. Like rabbits, in cages, they were on display for others' viewing pleasure and she hated that as well. What she lacked in height she made up for in attitude. Tinuke had a sharp tongue and used it at will. Usually to cut other children and even adults down to size. She was afraid of no one and earned the name "baby lawyer" from Big Mummy. Tinuke kept her emotional shield up all the time. It was exhausting, but the alternative for her, being vulnerable, was worse. She promised herself from an early age that she would never again put herself in a position where someone could hurt her.

While Atiunke was absorbed in her sober reflections, little Ella had found her and was climbing up the tree to join her. When Tinuke noticed Ella's attempt to climb the huge tree, she shouted down at her. "Don't be silly; you are going to hurt yourself!"

Ella didn't stop climbing and was obviously struggling, as her arms were not strong enough, but she gave it her best. Tinuke watched intently as Ella's facial expressions gave her away; she could hardly reach the first branch. Tinuke wondered why this obviously sheltered little girl would make such an effort to get to her, but she pretended not to care, as usual. However, she couldn't resist glancing down every few seconds to watch Ella's progress. Ella finally made it to the first branch and Tinuke cheered and rooted for her, albeit silently. Many years later, when looking back at the event, Ella had remained lost as to what spurred her on to make such an effort to get up the tree. She just knew she had to make it up that tree or die trying.

By the time she reached the fourth branch where Tinuke was sitting, Ella was battered and bruised, her clothes torn, her new shoes terribly scuffed. But Ella had the widest grin on her face. Tinuke couldn't believe it!

When Ella settled on the branch after the climb, Tinuke asked her, "Why did you go through all of that?" Ella had no idea until years later that her response would mean so much to Tinuke and would eventually define their friendship. She tried to smile a little, as she was still a bit winded from the climb, and said simply, "I choose you. Will you be my friend?"

Tinuke struggled with her emotions. Ella's words kept repeating in her head. No one had ever chosen her before; it was an amazing thing. It was like Ella was releasing Tinuke from her self-imposed prison. Being vulnerable was her greatest fear, but she didn't think she could bluster her way through this one. She had to decide — all or nothing.

She took a deep breath and said: "YES, yes I will be your friend."

Tinuke had been scared, but she took the plunge, one she never regretted. Ella had proven to be a gift from God. The two little girls had forged a "best friends forever" friendship that day, high up in that tree. This friendship transcended all; they had become sisters. No one could come between Ella and Tinuke. Ella had spread her sunshine around and Tinuke had always been there to defend and attack on her behalf. Anyone who crossed Ella's path did so at their own peril; Atinuke was up in arms immediately. Ella had troubles of her own trying to settle into a new life. She had come from a conventional family, with a Mum and Dad who loved her and loved each other. But their utopian life had been ended by a drunk driver. Both Ella's parents were the only children of their parents and had no known relatives; so with the accident, she suddenly became a ward of the state. Ella had handled this change with such grace. No one except Tinuke knew she cried herself to sleep every night for almost a year. Tinuke just pretended not to hear.

Under Ella's amazing friendship, Tinuke also blossomed. All the hard edges she had built up slowly melted away. She was no longer described as a "keg of gunpowder ever ready to explode." She became warm and caring. She was able to love others because she too was loved. The friendship between

Ella and Tinuke grew even stronger when they both attended a Christian meeting, and a few of them from school gave their lives to Christ. Their friendship went through their teenage years, university and even Ella's marriage. Tinuke was always happy for her friend.

When Ella fell in love with Femi, Tinuke gave him a "once over" and gave her blessing. It was no wonder, of course, that she had been Ella's chief bridesmaid at her wedding. Now Femi was like her brother, and Tinuke was godmother to the boys. FJ and Tope loved Aunty Tinuke as much as they loved their parents. She was the best aunt ever, FJ often declared. Atinuke had a very successful career as a teacher. She enjoyed what she did, and always made it a point to look out for girls and boys like herself and Ella who had those empty eyes. Her students loved her. When it came to relationships, though, Tinuke had never been interested. Many guys came along, but she always gently turned them down. Whenever anyone asked her to describe her ideal man, she always replied, "God is preparing him somewhere, so I really can't say, but when I meet him. I'll know him."

Chapter 8

OR Tambo International Airport, Johannesburg

SOUTH AFRICA

D eji couldn't believe they were boarding the plane. His mind couldn't handle all that had happened in the last hour. There had been a drama with two ladies insisting after they had been checked-in that they couldn't fly that day anymore. The flight had been delayed because they had to remove their luggage from the plane. The airline officials had rushed them into the plane after a lot of pleading and arguments. Femi was still spaced out as he squeezed into his economy class seat, so he just obeyed whatever Deji told him to do. He was like a zombie, half oblivious of what was going on. Deji's heart was broken for his friend.

As they buckled their seat belts, Deji gave him an update from Tinuke. "I spoke to Tinuke, and she has arrived at the hospital. She is with the boys. The doctors are not telling her much about Ella because she isn't a relative."

Deji told his friend the truth. He wasn't going to make the mistake of lying to him again or withholding any information. The truth made it worse, though; with no information, it was difficult not to imagine the worst. Outwardly, and to his credit, Femi had seemed to keep his composure. He had wiped his tears. His eyes, however, were like a mirror into his soul. They looked empty. Deji jabbed him with his elbow across their seat hand rest. "Hey bro, hang in there, okay? Let's make the best of it for the next six hours." Femi nodded absentmindedly.

The plane began to taxi and for a moment there was a peaceful silence, and in a few minutes, they were off the ground. Deji looked down as the ground disappeared underneath. Femi seemed okay, at least until the plane took off.

Deji had no idea what triggered the next set of events. From nowhere, Femi let out a deep, painful, almost guttural sound. Deji could see other passengers in their cabin begin to look in their direction.

Deji tried to calm Femi down. "Bro, calm down!" but Femi wouldn't let up and continued his howl of pain.

One of the cabin crew members began making his way toward them as passengers began to complain and some even began to panic. They had no idea what was going on. The flight attendant, who looked senior, arrived at their seat, clearly agitated.

He asked with a loud whisper, "What is the matter with him? Do we need to restrain him?"

Deji stifled the irritation welling up within him, stood up and touched the man's shoulder, and replied gently, "No, please don't. He isn't dangerous."

The attendant gave an audible sigh. "Should I call to see if there is a doctor on the flight?"

"A doctor may help," Deji replied, "but his pain isn't physical."

The attendant was now confused and spoke slightly sternly. "Look, sir, your friend is making other passengers very uncomfortable. He is going to have to keep quiet or we may have to declare him a hostile passenger."

Deji looked around him and he could see the unease in the faces on his fellow passengers. He remembered something his mother always said when anyone stared at her or made ugly comments. *Deji my boy, people are afraid of what they do not know or understand.* This sentence, one of the many wise statements from this mother, rang through Deji's mind. This philosophy made it easy for her to forgive people who were cruel to her. It's was a pity they could not look past her physical deformity. With that in mind, Deji turned to the passengers in his cabin and spoke as clearly and as loudly as he could over the sound of his friend's wail. He prayed in his heart. He knew that this was going to be the most difficult sales pitch of his life, and he needed all the help he could get.

"Good afternoon, all. Here beside me is my friend and brother. I have known him all my life. We have been best friends since he helped me fight off a bunch of bullies that had been making my life a living hell way back in primary school. He is that kind of guy. Well, this afternoon we got a call that his wife, the love of his life of over 15 years, was involved in an accident and she is in a coma. We haven't gotten any more information, so we don't have exact details of her current status. He has been strong for the past two hours. I think he has broken under the pressure. Please just be patient with him while he composes himself. I pray none of you will ever have to go through what he is going through now."

Deji looked around the cabin and thought to himself, *Wow! Mum was right.*" He could see understanding instead of fear in the eyes of the other passengers. He saw tears in the eyes of a woman a few rows behind them. Femi wasn't a crazy stranger anymore; he was their friend or even a brother in pain, just like anyone else they loved. The cabin was silent save the continuous wail from Femi. The crew member, not sure of how to react, patted Deji's shoulder and walked away. Deji's eyes caught an elderly gentleman across the aisle.

The man asked in a raised voice. "Is your friend a Christian? Would he mind if we prayed for him?"

Deji responded, "He and his wife are devout Christians. Yes, I guess you can pray if you want to." The man replied, "I want to. I will pray for a miracle for his wife and peace for your friend, and that he will feel God's comfort around him at this time and his heart will be at peace. Also, that God will go before him to make every crooked path straight and God will be glorified in this situation. I also ask anyone else who cares to join me to do so."

The old man, who had been standing as he spoke, gently sat down.

Deji noticed many passengers bowing their heads to pray. He sat down and buckled his seat belt once again as tears came to his eyes, humbled at the wonderful picture of humanity and love. Femi, still beside him, oblivious to all the excitement he had caused, continued to wail softly. But soon Deji noticed something. Rather, he felt something – a warm and cosy feeling all around him. Slowly Femi's sobs began to subside and, seemingly miraculously, he fell asleep. His face wasn't strained. He looked as peaceful as a baby in his mother's arms. *God hears prayers after all*, Deji thought. *He seems to be on duty today; maybe it was just my prayers he didn't answer.* Femi slept for the rest of the flight.

Chapter 9

Tinuke and Wale

Tinuke pulled herself back from Wale quickly in embarrassment. *What were you thinking of, Tinuke? This guy will think you are crazy or something. Imagine hugging a total stranger like that.* In her mind though, he didn't seem quite like a stranger. *I blame the exhaustion and panic of the last two hours. I was desperate for some sort of comfort.* She tried to calm herself down. Wale just continued to stare. The minute she pulled away, he missed her already and felt instantly bereft. He almost wished he could tell her what was in his heart—*Come back to me!* —but he didn't. He looked away slightly to allow her to compose herself.

Wale said to her gently, "You've got to stop thanking me. Anyone else would have done the same thing."

She shook her head and said, "No, not everyone. Thank you very much. I don't even want to think of what could have happened to the boys if it was an evil person that had stopped to 'help' as you did. But God was watching over them, and he sent you."

Why is she looking at me like I am someone special? Wale shook himself free from the fantasy and said, "God doesn't use people like me. I was just in the right place at the right time."

Tinuke frowned in confusion. What did he mean by *people like me?* "I hear what you say, but you see, God doesn't need your permission to use you." She smiled.

Wale was spellbound by her 1000-watt smile; a smile that seemed to begin from her soul and light up every inch of her face. He could have continued staring at her all day, but the boys were getting impatient and demanded attention.

Wale and Tinuke led them to the waiting room chairs while still giving each other surreptitious glances. They got the boys some snacks and when they had eaten, they seemed ready to sleep. Tinuke held Tope in her arms while Wale allowed FJ to use his thighs as a pillow. The boys dozed off immediately. All was quiet in the waiting room, save the nurses chatting quietly behind the reception desk. It seemed a quiet evening in the hospital. Or maybe it was just quiet in this waiting room. As Wale and Tinuke began to sink into their thoughts, the quiet calm was broken by the entrance of a doctor in surgical scrubs.

The doctor was an elderly gentleman probably in his 60s, with a full head of black hair not usually found in persons of that age. As he approached, he reminded Tinuke of Santa Claus with his pot belly and fatherly look. She was quite astonished when he walked up to them and asked brusquely, without any preliminaries,

"Has the husband arrived yet?"

It was Tinuke who responded to his query. "He is on his way and will be here in a few hours. How is she?"

"Are you a relative", the Dr asked.

" Err . . . not quite" Tinuke found herself stammering.

This doctor's attitude is unnerving. Besides, I am Ella's sister in a way, thought Tinuke. The doctor seemed peeved by her response and obviously not in the mood to be questioned by a non-relative. He was quite gruff. "Since you are not sure of who you are, when her husband arrives, let me know immediately. I knock off at 7:00 in the morning. I would like to see him before I go."

With this statement he turned around and walked off, leaving Wale and Tinuke stunned, with their mouths open.

"Wow!" remarked Wale, "that was rude."

"I thought the same thing," Tinuke said. "He didn't even wait for us to ask any questions!" Tinuke huffed, "He needs to work on his manners. It is unacceptable!!" and she squared her shoulders. "You look really cute when you are angry." Wale blurted out. *Oh no! Did I say that out loud?* Tinuke turned to look at him with the same look she had just given the doctor whilst he was retreating.

"I am so sorry," Wale said, trying to look appropriately contrite.

"Sorry for what, exactly?" Tinuke asked. "Sorry that you think I am cute?"

Wale was confused. How does one respond to that? She was still staring at him with fire in her eyes. Oh my God, she was probably not into casual jokes!

But just then Tinuke burst into laughter. "Gotcha!"

Wale couldn't believe the naughty girl was pulling his leg! His laughter was part humor, part relief. "You got me, indeed," Wale said.

"Sorry, I love to tease, and I needed to laugh a bit," Tinuke said. "I've cried too much today. Ella is not just my friend; she is like my sister. If anything happened to her, I don't know what I'd do." She continued in a sober tone. "She is the closest thing I have to family. I am so scared right now." Tinuke burst into tears.

Wale didn't think twice. He reached out and pulled her close, as much as he could with the boys wedged between them, and held her tight. He wished he could take away the pain. He would have done anything to stop her tears. He couldn't. Her sobs eventually subsided.

"I am so sorry for falling apart like that," she sniffed, and she tried to smile.

He caught a glimpse of it, and he wished he could make her smile all the time. He realized suddenly he wanted to be the one that made her happy. The thought made him scared. *This can't be happening.* He felt like he was free falling and couldn't stop. There was just something about her. *Well, just for tonight. By morning we may never see each other again.* Tinuke was thinking along the same lines. *What is this thing I'm feeling? I'm not a kid, what's this heart fluttering going on in my chest?* She decided she would just let the night play out and be ready to face reality in the morning. With the same decision made by both, unknown to each other, they relaxed.

Tinuke began to share memories of her childhood, how she met Ella, and her years in the orphanage. She spoke about the struggles she'd had growing up, being so much smaller than her mates. She was the one in the corner at parties, and nobody believed she was as old as she claimed. She had to be twice as tough and fight twice as hard to be respected in her career, teaching in a primary school. Some of the Grade 7 children were bigger than she was! Wale listened. The more he heard her speak, the more he thought, *I want to be with this woman. I want to fight all those bullies. I want to be a hero for her.* Tinuke felt like a heavy load had been lifted off her chest.

She remarked, "Wow! I am sure I have just spoken more to you in one night than I must have anybody else save Ella. But I have to say; it felt good. Thank you for listening. I wish I could give you your ear back!"

"My ear?" Wale asked, genuinely confused.

"You know," Tinuke said, grinning mischievously. "Considering I just talked it off! I talked your ear off." Again she laughed . . . a sweet belly laugh. The laugh was so rich and so genuine, and at that moment Wale knew he was lost.

He joined her in laughing, not because the joke was that great, but because her laughter made him want to laugh. And because it was for one night only, he laughed and laughed till tears ran down his cheeks. They both sighed contentedly and sat in companionable silence.

Then she broke the silence when she asked, "Would you like to stretch your legs a bit? My little boy is now like a heavy weight on my legs. Let's drop them gently. Luckily they both sleep very deeply."

Wale didn't mind the boys, he loved holding them near, but he knew he would do whatever this lady suggested. So he adjusted FJ until he was spread across three seats and looked as comfortable as possible. They stood up and stretched, then walked around the waiting room never moving too far from the boys.

"Well," Tinuke began again. "I have told you all about myself; it's only fair you share about yourself; that's the rule."

Wale responded, "The rule, huh? Well, I haven't read the book, so it doesn't apply to me." He was getting the hang of the teasing, he thought to himself.

"No way, Mister, you are not getting off that easily!" Tinuke insisted. "Tell me about yourself."

"Okay, okay, my name is Wale Ojo," Wale started, quite reluctantly. "I own an IT company. My favorite food is pounded yam and efo eiro. I have no favorite color, I have no favorite song, I have no best friend, and that's about it." Wale tried to exhume an air of finality in a weak attempt to ward off any further questions.

"Wow! Mister Wale, that was a horrible bio," Tinuke said as she laughed. "You haven't told me much and the little you've said is quite depressing. No offense." She said as her eyes twinkled.

"None taken," Wale replied.

"Ok, since you don't know how to play this game, I'll help you. I'll ask the questions and you answer," Tinuke said in the tone of an instructor.

Wale began to feel tense. What had he gotten himself into? He didn't know how to backtrack. He was suddenly afraid.

"First question. What makes you happy?" Tinuke said. *You,* Wale thought to himself instantly. "Work," he said out loud. "I love what I do. It makes me happy."

"Hmm ... work, okay," Tinuke said, nodding her head gently. "Who is the most important person to you in this world?" *You,* he thought again, but then a picture of his grandma came clearly into his mind. And he felt the sadness welling up again.

He replied gruffly, "No one!" He didn't realize he had barked at her until he looked up and saw the shocked look on her face. He had responded more harshly than he intended, but he was afraid of the emotions the mental picture of his grandma evoked, and he was terrified of breaking down in front of his lady. So, he settled for an emotion he could handle. Anger.

He faced Tinuke and said, "Why don't you just mind your own business!" He turned and walked out of the waiting room, out of the hospital, and into the street. He needed some air.

Wale looked around in surprise. It was already dark. Why tonight? Why did he remember Mama so much tonight!? He wanted to forget! He wanted this heavy load in his heart and conscience gone. But he couldn't escape.

He yelled to no one, "LEAVE ME ALONE, PLEASE! I AM SORRRYYY! I DIDN'T MEAN FOR HER TO GET HURT! JUDGE ME NOW OR LEAVE ME!"

He momentarily considered jumping into a nearby river and ending it all. He couldn't bear this torment any longer. This fear of pending judgment, the guilt, and this darkness shrouded him all the time. Except just now when he was with her. His mind wandered to the boys and the freedom they had in the love of their parents, how confident they seemed, and he thought of the lady he just met, so beautiful, so confident, so brave, facing her own wars every day and ready to love the next minute. He wished he had another life, a second chance. He sat down on the grass and began to cry from his heart. "God Almighty, forgive me, please, I will do anything you ask, please forgive me. I didn't mean to hurt her! I didn't. Please forgive or judge me, but please do it now." He sat in the grass outside the hospital and cried for a long time. When he stood up, he knew one thing. Something had to change, and that lady in there was somehow the key.

Chapter 10

Murtala Mohammed International Airport

LAGOS

The plane touched down in Lagos at exactly 8:50 pm. Deji was dreading having to wake Femi up. They still had to go through Immigration and somehow find their way through the dreaded Lagos traffic. He was tempted to pray to this God again, since He seemed to be available today. But he didn't. He figured God could see what was happening anyway and if He felt like He wanted to do something, He would.

Deji wondered how the next few hours were going to be. He waited until the last minute, just as the plane was taxiing to a stop, before he decided to wake Femi up.

He shook him gently and said, "My guy, we are here."

Femi slowly opened his eyes. Deji explained that they had just landed in Lagos. Femi looked temporarily uncertain of his surroundings. As reality dawned on him again, his face crumpled, but he didn't break down. Deji heaved a sigh of relief.

Femi simply said, "God is in control." It seemed he had resigned himself to whatever awaited them when they got to the hospital. To Deji, he looked like a different person.

Deji got their luggage from the overhead compartment and prepared to join the line and exit the plane as quickly as possible. The older gentleman who had offered to pray earlier came up to where they were and greeted them.

He said, "When you get past Immigration, show any of the security officers my card." He handed the card to Deji. "He will take you to the head of my personal security team, and one of my drivers will take you with armed escort anywhere you need to go to in Lagos. You will not be delayed by traffic or checkpoints. My security team has government clearance documents."

Deji's mouth dropped open, and Femi just looked confused. Looking dazed, he said, " Sir, do I know you?"

The man replied, "We are brothers. I heard you were in a hurry, and I just want to help."

Deji offered up thanks profusely, at the same time wondering why a man who seemed obviously powerful flew in economy class. Well, this wasn't the time to question. He and Femi prepared to leave the plane.

The head of the cabin crew met up with them and said, "Follow me."

He turned and began to run. Deji and Femi didn't ask any questions; they just picked up their pace and ran right alongside him. He took them right to the front of the immigration queue. It seemed they were expected. Their passports were stamped in seconds and they were off to the exit.

The cabin crew official brushed aside their thanks and said, "When you get to the arrivals, look for a tall gentleman in uniform—he is the head of security for General Johnson."

Femi stopped in his tracks. "Wait! What?! I don't understand. Who are you people? Why are you all doing this?"

The cabin crew official replied as he turned to go, "Ask your friend here, and remember, we are all praying for your wife."

As the arrival door opened, Deji and Femi were approached by a man in uniform.

He asked, "Guests of General Johnson from Johannesburg?"

Deji and Femi could only nod. It was all happening so fast.

"Please follow me," the man said, as he turned and hurried down the hall. Deji and Femi followed. If the situation wasn't so dire, Deji would have laughed at all the running they had done so far.

As they arrived at the special car park, they saw a black SUV with tinted glass, surrounded by four large motorbikes. The vehicle already had its flashing lights on, a sure way of telling all other cars on the roads to move out of the way. They jumped in, the driver turned the siren on, and they sped off while Deji gave the driver the name of the hospital in Lekki phase 1. Deji and Femi were still gobsmacked, and it all seemed surreal as they were whisked out of the airport faster than either of them thought was ever possible.

Femi finally found his voice and asked, "Deji, what did you do? How did you get all this done?" Deji swallowed. He had just experienced a series of miracles, and he didn't know how to process it all. He knew all of this was beyond him. He couldn't speak.

He just deflected by saying, "I said I'll tell you all about it later. Right now, we need to call Tinuke and find out how Ella is."

Chapter 11

The Lekki Hospital

LAGOS

Once Wale had made up his mind, he went back into the hospital. As he walked through the door of the waiting room, he saw Tinuke pacing up and down by the chairs where the boys were sleeping, a worried look on her face. She looked up and their eyes met. The relief that washed over her face made Wale feel so guilty.

Tinuke sighed loudly and ran to him. "I am so sorry. I talk too much, I know. Please forgive me. I was scared you had gone. I would have followed you out, but I couldn't leave the boys, and Femi called asking for an update. Are you okay? I didn't mean any offense."

Wale was puzzled. She shouldn't apologize to him, but here she was doing just that when for all intents and purposes, he was the one being silly. *What kind of woman is this?* Wale thought. Tinuke's voice interrupted his thoughts. "I was just praying for God to keep you. You left without your car keys. It's so late at night and the streets are not always safe."

She went on speaking without a pause. *Hmm, she was worried about me?* Wale thought, feeling quite humbled. *If I am going to be judged, this must be my judgment, to meet the missing piece of your life and not be able to have her.* He still hadn't said a word. He led her gently to their seats. She followed, not saying anything further. Wale sat her down and took a few minutes to compose himself, and then he began to tell his story. He started from the very beginning. He spoke about his childhood with his parents, his dad's abandonment, and his mum's suicide. Then he got to the story of his grandma, life with her, meeting up with the gang, and finally her death. He didn't leave anything out. He didn't look at Tinuke. He kept his face turned to his lap. Even when she reached out to hold his hand, he didn't stop talking. This dam had been bottled up for years and he needed a release. She knew it. He told her about his life after he ran away from the village. He had gone to the city and roamed the streets for days, not knowing anyone. He still had no idea how he had survived. There were days he thought he was going to die of hunger. If not hunger, then the sickness that ravaged his body by being exposed to malaria mosquitoes that feasted on his blood at night. If not that, then the heat from the blazing sun. Somehow, he had survived it all.

He told her of a chance event when he helped a man who had an accident. The stranger took him in and changed his life, and sponsored him through school, where he found he had a talent for business. He started his own business while in University, opening a barbering salon and selling drinks at the same location. It became a very popular hangout for undergraduates. His fellow students had no idea he was the owner of the trendy spot. They assumed he was a student working to make ends meet while in school. That was just the beginning. Now he had a full-scale business empire, running multiple companies. It seemed everything he touched turned to gold. But every morning after a restless night of hardly any sleep, the first thing that popped up in his head was Mama Tayo's voice. "Murderer! God will judge you!" The same voice every day for the past 15 years.

"My life seems so perfect on the outside, but honestly, Tinuke, I am a dead man walking. I feel meeting you tonight is my judgment," Wale said in a quiet shaky voice.

Tinuke looked confused "How?" she asked.

Before he could reply, the waiting room doors burst open and two men rushed in. Tinuke looked up and shrieked. "FEMI!" She jumped up from her seat as Femi and Deji ran toward her. Confused chatter mixed with tears and hugs as each tried to get a word in. When they all finally calmed down, Tinuke spoke up. "No word yet. But please go in and ask for Dr Adams. He said he wanted to see you once you got in." Femi turned and hurried away. Deji and Tinuke resumed talking, and Wale seemed to fade into the background.

Watching as Deji and Tinuke talked, he couldn't help but notice how Deji's hands were on Tinuke's back for a bit too long. Wale knew he had no right to feel jealous, but he did anyway. Why was he holding her like that? What's with the extended physical contact? Then suddenly, the thought popped into his head. What if they had something going on? As these thoughts assailed him, Wale realized he never even asked her if she was dating someone. In his mind, he had claimed Tinuke for his own without even considering the possibility she may not be available. *Oh well, I knew I couldn't have her anyway.* But then he looked at both of them again and his irritation with Deji resurfaced. He had to confess that they both looked good together and were obviously at ease with one another.

The young man in question was tall with broad shoulders, very well dressed in his obviously high-end casual black shirt and black trousers. He had a square jaw and deep, steady eyes. His head was closely shaved, and he was sporting an extremely well-trimmed beard. *Hmm . . . a B and B*, Wale thought to himself, referring to the Bald and Bearded look. It was the trending look among men these days. According to the ladies in his office, it exuded strength and power. They thought men who sported the look were all so handsome. Wale had to admit, albeit grudgingly, that this Deji fellow held it all well together. His thoughts trailed off again as he continued to observe them. *Why is he still holding her?*

Tinuke turned around and said, "Wale, please come over, let me introduce you." The smile she cast his way wiped away all the irritation. Wale walked toward them and stretched out his hand in greeting.

Deji pulled him into a hug and said "My brother, thanks so much for what you did for these boys today. Thank you very much indeed."

Startled, Wale tried to brush it aside, but Deji insisted and repeated his effusive thanks.

"I apologize for Femi's abruptness. Once he sees Ella with his own eyes, I am sure he will thank you, too."

Wale looked slightly embarrassed and said, "Look, it's not a problem."

He turned to Tinuke and said, not quite looking in her eyes, "I guess I should be going now, Tinuke, I can see you are in safe hands." At this, he gave a watery smile.

Tinuke looked up at him in surprise. "Leave? Please don't go." Tinuke caught herself mid-sentence; she didn't want to sound desperate. "Umm . . . I mean, if you don't have to." And then she looked at him full in the face, her eyes speaking the words she couldn't say and hoping he understood. Wale sighed. He knew he could not leave, not when she had asked him to stay.

He said softly, "I am here as long as you want me."

Deji noticed this exchange in silence. But he didn't miss a thing. They spoke as if there was no one else in the room. He could have been on planet Mars, for all these two cared. The look in their eyes was unmistakable. If not that the situation was so dire, he would have begun teasing Tinuke mercilessly. He always jokingly called her "Madam small but mighty." She hated it, but he always teased her anyway, even though he knew how much she couldn't stand her height being the butt of some joke. *Hmm, so the iron lady has fallen?* Deji thought. He found it very amusing, but he was genuinely happy for her. It was just sad that he and Tinuke had never had romantic chemistry. The best friends of the couple becoming a couple as well. It would have been so easy. But it just wasn't meant to be. They had never seen themselves as anything more than friends. They were as close as any brother or sister, but nothing more.

The three of them talked for what seemed like hours, each of them narrating their own experiences of this extremely stressful day. They were whispering, trying not to disturb the kids who had fallen asleep again after the initial excitement of seeing their dad. They eventually heard footsteps behind them. They turned and saw Femi coming toward them as white as a sheet. They all rose as one, each afraid to ask, but desperate to know.

"She survived the surgery; she is going to be alright," Femi said.

At that, Femi collapsed in a heap and cried and cried, tears of relief, tears of gratitude. Deji couldn't hold himself either. He hugged his best friend and allowed the tears to fall. He had been holding it together for Femi all this while. Tinuke joined in, and Femi and Tinuke began to praise God in the Yoruba language, extolling His greatness and His might and thanking him for His mercy in this situation.

Deji knew that God had moved on their behalf in so many ways. He saw His hand and he was awed and so humbled. Instead of gratitude to Him, though, he felt resentful, but kept it well contained. He was very happy for Femi and Ella. When Femi was able, they began to ply him with questions. What had happened? What could have caused a perfectly healthy woman to just slump in this manner?

"A brain aneurysm," Femi responded. "It ruptured."

"What?" they all inquired in unison.

Then Tinuke asked "How did she get that? Is it like cancer?"

"Not really," Femi responded. "That's what the Dr wanted to know. It could be hereditary or lifestyle-related, or even a single event can cause it. I told him about the fall she had a few weeks ago. Remember? Where she had to get stitches? Apparently, that could also be the cause."

It was Deji's turn to note, "But she was fine after that incident."

Femi nodded and said, "He says there are symptoms like headaches, dizziness, and nausea, but sometimes there may be none. Ella didn't mention anything to me about any symptoms, so I don't know what to think. They had to do what is called a surgical clipping. They removed a section of the skull and a metal clip was placed on the opening of an aneurysm to cut off the blood flow."

"Wow, poor Ella, but thank God for His hand of mercy in all this," Tinuke said, raising her hands to the Heavens.

Deji was stunned and couldn't hold back. He exploded "Thank God? Thank God? Like, seriously, what did He do? Where was He when Ella fell and bumped her head two weeks ago? Where was He when she almost killed herself and the kids while driving? Do you know how dangerous that was? Where was He then?"

Tinuke turned to Deji and said softly, "He was there, Deji. He was there when she fell; the fall could have killed her. He was there when she was driving with the kids; she was able to park the car safely before she passed out, that was His mercy, He was there protecting the kids when he made Wale stop and check on them, that was His mercy. Can you imagine if miscreants were the ones who got to the scene first? How do you explain your trip here? From beginning to the end, God's grace and mercy are evident. Deji, even you cannot deny it. You saw God on this trip. Bad things happen, yes, but God doesn't abandon us. He promised He will never leave us nor forsake us. Life or death, God was with Ella. His mercy was extended to those of us she would have left behind."

Deji was silent. He knew deep in his heart what she had said was true. But he could not get past his own personal hurt.

"Then why?" Deji cried. "Why didn't he answer me when I called? Why did he not hear my cry? I was only seven years old. She didn't have to die. Your God could have saved her!" Deji was now bent over sobbing.

It was Femi's turn to comfort him. Deji was so embarrassed, but he couldn't help himself. A dam of grief had been released. It seemed like his mother had just died, not that she died over 30 years ago.

"She had believed in God, and He just let her die! Now today He is performing miracles everywhere. Where was He when I needed him all those years ago? Where was He?!" Deji cried.

Femi knelt down before his friend of many years and said, "I don't know why Aunty died that day. There are some things we can never fully understand on this side of heaven, why some people are healed, and some are not. Why bad things happen. I wish she didn't have to go. But you see, all of us on earth have our lives already written out from beginning to end. Aunty had just finished hers."

Deji looked at him with anger and said "Finished? With a 7-year-old boy without a mother?"

Femi took this outburst in stride and said quietly, "I miss her too, Deji. But one thing I know—God loves you. The devil used the opportunity of your grief to sow a lie that God doesn't care. The Bible says that He has a plan for each of us. And He has loved us with an everlasting love. Deji, God loves you. How do you know all this drama wasn't for you to see that He can be anywhere and do anything? If God took Aunty home, it was because it was her time, not because He didn't want to help, and it wasn't to punish you. My brother, I have watched you carry this anger toward God for far too long. I think it's time bro . . . Come home. Aunty didn't spend all those nights on her weak knees praying for both of us for you to hate God forever."

Deji looked at his friend. "Why are you telling me all this now?"

Femi closed his eyes for a second and answered truthfully. "I should have spoken to you sooner, I admit, but somehow I felt the time was never right. But today, as I faced the fear of losing Ella, I realized something. I would have been totally crushed, but deep down I knew that death on earth was not the end, I would still see her again at the resurrection. But you, my brother, if anything happens to you now with this anger in your heart toward God, then the devil would have won. And that I could not stand. Forgive me for being quiet so long. But look here, life is full of ups and some hard downs, but there are always blessings in the dark. My brother, can't you see?"

It was such a strange thing to say, but somehow Deji understood it. And as he pondered, it was as if the eyes of his understanding were suddenly illuminated; blessings in the dark, that had been the story of his life.

Moving into Femi's neighborhood and becoming friends, their two mums becoming fast friends to the extent that when his mum died, Femi's mother took on the role of Deji's mother with all her heart. It wasn't the same, but it was nice having your best friend's mum cheer louder than anyone when you climbed on stage, whether Daddy could make it or not. Femi's mum was there right in front. He knew love, and he had never been sick a day in his life, something he had always taken for granted, but now he saw it for what it was—a blessing in the dark. Even when he couldn't see, God was showering him with blessings. He worked at something he enjoyed and made good money. He was comfortable. He had good friends, a good life, blessings in the dark. He knew it was time to let all that anger go. God is good, and in that, there is no lie.

As he became convinced in his heart, he spoke it out in just a whisper, "God is good."

Femi didn't need anything else. He knew his brother was home.

Wale watched on in disbelief and partly in awe. He wondered about this God that Femi and Tinuke talked about. A God of love? A God that forgives? No! The God he knew didn't suffer fools, and he was a God of Judgement! He couldn't reconcile the two. Which one was the real God of the Bible? The one that had terrified him all these years? Or this one he was hearing about this day? He got up and left the room. Tinuke saw him, and got up and followed him out. She watched as he sat on a bench under a huge palm tree outside in the parking lot. She walked over quietly and sat down beside him. They sat in silence.

Tinuke knew that he needed some sort of help and she prayed to God there and then for the right words to say if any were needed.

After a few minutes, she asked quietly, "What did you mean earlier when you said I was your judgment?" Wale didn't respond immediately.

Then he said, "I knew God's punishment was coming. I have always known this." He paused to take a deep breath. "Today when I saw you, I wanted you in my life more than I have ever wanted anything else in this world. As we spent more time together, I knew I was falling in love with you." At this, Tinuke sucked in her breath. Wale didn't notice and he kept on speaking. "Tinuke, I do not pursue or encourage personal relationships, but when I met you, I knew I needed you. I also know we can never be together because no woman like you will want to be attached to a murderer — someone like me, with a curse on his head. So, you see? The one thing I want more than anything, I can never have. That is judgment.

A life of misery like I have never known because before today I never yearned for anything. I just existed. Now I will live the rest of my days yearning for what I can never have."

Leaning forward, his elbows on his knees, Wale said all this without looking at her. Tinuke was so silent, he almost thought she had left him. Then he felt her tiny arms wrap around him. She could barely get her arms around his huge torso. He stiffened, not daring to move, in the event this was a dream. He could feel dampness on the back of his shirt. *Was she crying?*

"Tinuke?" Wale tried to turn around, but she wouldn't let go; she just held on to him. Silently weeping.

Finally, she said, "Wale, have you ever asked God to forgive you for your part in your grandma's demise?"

"I have!" Wale cried out, relieved that he could even talk about it with another human being. "I ask every day for His forgiveness. I never meant for her to get hurt, believe me, Tinuke. I wish I could go back in time, run faster than they did, stand up to those boys, tell them no. I never meant to hurt her . . . I loved her." Wale began to sob. *Not again*, he thought. He had cried more today than he had in his 35 years of life, but he sobbed nonetheless.

Tinuke said quietly, "Please let me quote a portion of the Bible for you. Please listen to God's word. 1 John 1:9: 'If we say we have no sin, we deceive ourselves and the truth is not in us, but if we humbly confess our sin, God is faithful and just and will forgive us our sin and cleanse us from all unright-eousness.'" The words were like a balm for his tortured soul.

Wale asked, "Can that be for me? My sin is too great."

Tinuke continued, "Isaiah 1:18 says, 'Come now, let us rea-son together, says the Lord, though your sins are like scarlet, they will be as white as snow; though they are red as crimson, they will become like wool."

After a pause, Tinuke continued, "Wale, God is in the business of cleansing and restoring. He forgave you the first time you asked. The devil just used your ignorance of God's nature to deceive you into thinking that He won't forgive. That's not the way God is."

Wale could not believe all he was hearing.

Tinuke didn't stop. "Isaiah 43:25 says 'I, even I am He who blots out your transgressions, for my own sake and remembers your sins no more.'" The scriptures seemed to be flowing from her. She silently thanked God for Aunty Pat, their Sunday School teacher, who had insisted they all learned Bible verses every Sunday, sometimes at the threat of punishment.

"Is that in the Bible too?" Wale asked incredulously.

"Yes, it is, Wale," she replied softly. "God loves you. He wants you to enjoy this life He has given you. He loves you, and He has forgiven you. He doesn't hold your past against you. Jesus has already paid the price to make you clean and righteous."

This was all too much for Wale. Tinuke could see he was getting overwhelmed and assured him, saying. "Don't worry; we have time. We will go through all the scriptures you need to understand salvation and the price that was paid for you. For now, just be convinced. You have been forgiven and God loves you, Wale. Can you please now turn and face me?" Wale did and saw her, her eyes bright with even more unshed tears, but this time she had a smile on her face.

"Are you okay?", Tinuke asked.

Wale nodded and replied, "I will be. Thank you, Tinuke."

"You are welcome, my friend" Tinuke replied, "Can I pray with you?"

As he nodded, she reached out and grabbed his hands and prayed. The most beautiful prayer of love for God he had ever heard. He wanted this relationship with God as well. He was convinced. And for the first time in his entire life, he said an 'amen' and knew God heard him. It warmed Wale's heart.

When the prayer was over, they walked hand in hand into the hospital. When they got to the waiting room, Femi, Deji, and the kids were gone, and there was a slight pandemonium, with nurses running all over the place. She heard beeps going off and an announcement made for Dr. Adams to report to the theatre.

Tinuke turned to the nearest nurse in panic. "Where are the gentlemen and the children that were here?"

The nurse took a second to think and said, "Oh, there was some development with the patient, and they rushed away to see her. She is on the second floor. Go up the stairs just at the end of this corridor, and turn right. Second door on your left."

Tinuke, scared and still holding onto Wale's hand, rushed in the direction the nurse had described. They went up the stairs to the next floor and turned right. There she saw a nurse looking rather formidable, scowling in front of a room with its door open. She could hear hushed giggling from the boys. She knew she was in the right place. Whatever development, Ella had to be in good shape if they were laughing, and she breathed a sigh of thanks.

She and Wale walked to the nurse quietly, almost as if they knew instinctively that this was not a woman to mess with. Tinuke practiced her best smile to woo this barrel of a woman. She politely asked the nurse if she could see the patient briefly.

The nurse turned to face Tinuke and Wale with a look of utter disdain. She retorted angrily, "This is not a guest house! My patient has just been released from the ICU. She needs peace and quiet to recover fully. The doctor said just close family for a few minutes, and a whole horde of people are in here already. No more!"

She waved her palm across the door for emphasis. Her raised voice must have alerted the occupants of the room because Fj bounced out and ran to Tinuke.

Jumping excitedly, he shouted, "Aunty Tinuke, Mummy is awake! Come and see!"

The nurse was about to respond when Deji came out as well, gave the nurse his famous winning smile. "Ma'am, I just want to say thank you once again for the amazing work you do. We understand your concern and we will soon be out of your hair, but your patient is urgently requesting the presence of her sister." He pointed at Tinuke standing beside Wale.

The nurse blushed and stammered. "Oh, okay. But she can't stay too long—hospital policy, you know" She giggled a little.

Deji smiled broadly. "We understand, Ma'am."

As Tinuke stepped up to go in, the nurse stopped her and asked, "Who is he?" pointing at Wale. "Family, too?"

Deji looked at Tinuke with raised eyebrow, she looked at the nurse squarely in the eye and said sweetly, "Yes! Yes, he is family too."

Wale stood up taller than his 6 feet 5 inches, and he couldn't believe this tiny dynamite. Well, he wanted to be family. Maybe she wanted it, too. He could only dare to hope.

In the room, Tinuke quietly and quickly hugged her friend the best she could and fought back the tears as she realized how easily this could have been a totally different scenario.

She whispered in Ella's ear as she could see the burning curiosity when she saw her come in with Wale.

"Don't worry, I'll give you the scoop", Tinuke said. Both ladies giggled in anticipation.

The nurse decided it was a good time to break up the party and ordered everyone out except for Femi, who was given a minute to say good night under the nurse's watchful eye. Everyone else was promptly ushered out of the room. Ella was slightly overwhelmed at this point. She hadn't fully understood all the story FJ and Tope were trying to give her about what had happened; all she knew was that Femi was here. Her Femi. All was right in her world. She noted as well that Deji looked different. She couldn't place it.

Meanwhile, Tinuke seemed to have grown a foot taller. Who was the hunk with her? Oh well, she would know soon enough. *Just one day in a coma and so many things had happened!* She laughed at her own not-so-funny joke as she succumbed to sleep.

Chapter 12

Back in the waiting room, Femi finally got a chance to interact with Wale properly. He thanked him again and again, even attempting to prostrate on the floor, a greeting reserved for elders and dignitaries among the Yoruba people of Nigeria. Wale would not let him. Regardless, Femi's thanks and appreciation was effusive.

"My brother, thank God that you were there to help us," Femi said.

To which Wale replied, "Thank God, indeed. Honestly though, it was I who needed the real help." As he said this, he glanced at Tinuke.

Femi laughed and said, "Thank God He helped both of us then!"

Deji and Tinuke and the kids chimed in and said "Amen! And amen!"

They all laughed. Deji and Tinuke decided to go and get everyone snacks from the canteen, and the kids went with them. It was now the early hours of the morning. It had been a long night for all of them.

Femi and Wale sat alone in companionable silence. Wale turned to Femi and asked a question he'd had on his mind ever since he walked into the hospital room and saw Femi on his knees at his wife's side.

"Femi, can I ask a question?" Wale asked.

"Sure, go ahead" Femi replied.

"Why her? Why Ella? How did you know she was the one? What is so special about her?" Wale asked.

Femi repeated the question to himself softly, thinking about how to respond. "How does a person become so important to you?"

Femi smiled thoughtfully. "One day at a time, my brother. One day at a time. I love Ella more today than I did the first day we met. You see, when I look at her, I not only see her gorgeous face. I see over 15 years of absolute dedication, tears, sweat, and sacrifice, not for herself but for me. Over 15 years of lifting me up so that I can breathe better, feel better, see better. Almost two decades, speaking into my life, praying for me, speaking me out of sadness, pulling me forcefully out of burning bushes, and taking the heat on her back for no other reason than she loves me. Crazy, isn't it? I see God's love for me through her eyes. When she stands, every other woman pales in comparison. From the minute I saw her when I was 17, it was her. It's always been her, and it will always be her. As for your other question, why Ella? My brother, the question is why me? And the answer to that real question is lost to me; all I know is that the God of heaven decided in His mercy to bless me with one of Earth's finest. I don't deserve her, but I'm so grateful. Why me? No idea."

As Femi was speaking, Wale looked up and saw Tinuke laughing with the kids and Deji. He stared at her. She looked at him, caught his eye, and gave him her 1 000-watt smile as she approached him. The smile held no reproach; just a promise of things to come. As Wale's heart literally skipped a beat, he thought to himself, *Why me?*